Third Class

Brad Slaight

A Samuel French Acting Edition

SAMUELFRENCH.COM
SAMUELFRENCH-LONDON.CO.UK

Copyright © 2013 by Brad Slaight
All Rights Reserved

THIRD CLASS is fully protected under the copyright laws of the United States of America, the British Commonwealth, including Canada, and all other countries of the Copyright Union. All rights, including professional and amateur stage productions, recitation, lecturing, public reading, motion picture, radio broadcasting, television and the rights of translation into foreign languages are strictly reserved.

ISBN 978-0-573-70235-8

www.SamuelFrench.com
www.SamuelFrench-London.co.uk

For Production Enquiries

United States and Canada
Info@SamuelFrench.com
1-866-598-8449

United Kingdom and Europe
Plays@SamuelFrench-London.co.uk
020-7255-4302

Each title is subject to availability from Samuel French, depending upon country of performance. Please be aware that *THIRD CLASS* may not be licensed by Samuel French in your territory. Professional and amateur producers should contact the nearest Samuel French office or licensing partner to verify availability.

CAUTION: Professional and amateur producers are hereby warned that *THIRD CLASS* is subject to a licensing fee. Publication of this play(s) does not imply availability for performance. Both amateurs and professionals considering a production are strongly advised to apply to Samuel French before starting rehearsals, advertising, or booking a theatre. A licensing fee must be paid whether the title(s) is presented for charity or gain and whether or not admission is charged. Professional/Stock licensing fees are quoted upon application to Samuel French.

No one shall make any changes in this title(s) for the purpose of production. No part of this book may be reproduced, stored in a retrieval system, or transmitted in any form, by any means, now known or yet to be invented, including mechanical, electronic, photocopying, recording, videotaping, or otherwise, without the prior written permission of the publisher. No one shall upload this title(s), or part of this title(s), to any social media websites.

For all enquiries regarding motion picture, television, and other media rights, please contact Samuel French.

MUSIC USE NOTE

Licensees are solely responsible for obtaining formal written permission from copyright owners to use copyrighted music in the performance of this play and are strongly cautioned to do so. If no such permission is obtained by the licensee, then the licensee must use only original music that the licensee owns and controls. Licensees are solely responsible and liable for all music clearances and shall indemnify the copyright owners of the play(s) and their licensing agent, Samuel French, against any costs, expenses, losses and liabilities arising from the use of music by licensees. Please contact the appropriate music licensing authority in your territory for the rights to any incidental music.

IMPORTANT BILLING AND CREDIT REQUIREMENTS

If you have obtained performance rights to this title, please refer to your licensing agreement for important billing and credit requirements.

THIRD CLASS was developed at the Young Conservatory of American Conservatory Theater in San Francisco, California.

CHARACTERS

Suggested: 12 students – 8f, 4m
Because of the number of scenes you can use more or less than the suggested cast.

SETTING

A modern High School

TIME

The present. The action of the play takes place over the course of a school year.

AUTHOR'S NOTES

The Set: The set can be as simple or complex as you wish to make it. In the script I have suggested using cubes that can be moved around and stacked to simulate settings for the individual scenes when needed. You may also consider using a "two color" set, which reflects your school colors.

Music: You could use contemporary transitional music between the scenes, as well as sound effects and mood music when needed in scenes.

Costumes: Basic modern school clothes and suggestive props

"The least of the work of learning is done in the classrooms."
– Thomas Merton (1915–1968)

OPENING

*(As the audience enters, they will see **BRIAN** onstage. He is sitting on a towel and wears sunglasses. It should seem like he is at the beach getting a tan and he might even put on suntan lotion at some point. When the show is ready to start, the audience lights will fade out, leaving only the stage lights.)*

*(**JESSICA** enters. She is dressed in new school clothes and wears a backpack. She spots **BRIAN** and crosses to him.)*

JESSICA. What are you doing?

BRIAN. What does it look like? I'm workin' on my tan.

JESSICA. Earth to Brian…summer break is over. It's the first day of school.

BRIAN. *(looks at watch)* Not yet. I still have eight more minutes of summer left…and I'm going to enjoy every last second of it.

JESSICA. In the school's courtyard?

BRIAN. If I did it anywhere else I would have to give up precious minutes in order to get to school on time.

JESSICA. You're crazy.

BRIAN. No, just squeezing every drop out of life that I can.

JESSICA. I think the sun has baked your brain.

BRIAN. With any luck it has…because I'm at my best when my mind is on fire!

(A bell is heard.)

JESSICA. You're going to be late.

BRIAN. I'll make it.

JESSICA. Don't say I didn't warn you.

*(**JESSICA** exits. **BRIAN** puts his sunglasses back on. Music comes up as the lights fade out.)*

Scene One

(Lights come up on stage and we discover a group of students talking among themselves in the school's hallway. **STEVEN** *and* **MELANIE** *make their way toward the stage;* **STEVEN** *carries a video camera and* **MELANIE** *holds a clipboard.)*

STEVEN. Come on, Melanie. Can't we start this next week or something?

MELANIE. No, I want to give the people their money's worth.

STEVEN. You really think the students here are going to buy this?

MELANIE. They buy hardcover yearbooks and this is way better.

STEVEN. But nobody's ever heard of a "video yearbook."

MELANIE. Lots of school's have them. It's just that nobody's ever made one here. That's why it will sell. Multiply every student in this school by $29.99 and we'll have a good chunk of our first year's college money next fall.

STEVEN. Yeah, but I'm the one doing all the work. I'm shooting, editing, and making the product. I should get more than 50%...

MELANIE. You're lucky to get that. It's my idea...and I have the hardest job.

STEVEN. What's that?

MELANIE. Directing it.

STEVEN. You mean telling me what to shoot.

MELANIE. Whatever.

STEVEN. You know teachers will never let us film in class.

MELANIE. We're not going to film anything in class. Most of the real stuff that kids care about happens outside of the classroom. In the halls, the parking lot, the bathrooms...

STEVEN. The bathrooms?

MELANIE. Places where we hang out together. Where we can be ourselves and say what's on our mind. That's where the real learning takes place at school.

STEVEN. The only thing I've learned in the bathroom is that they took the doors off the stalls because they don't trust us.

MELANIE. There are doors on the stalls in the Girls'.

STEVEN. Figures.

MELANIE. This is going to be better than anything any other school has ever made. We're going everywhere to make sure that our product is something everyone will want a copy of. We're going to make major bank.

STEVEN. We're probably going to get in major trouble.

(MELANIE notices all the students.)

MELANIE. This is good. We can start the project off with a general milling about scene...

STEVEN. General milling about?

MELANIE. We'll fade in on a group students...a beehive of activity...hanging out in the halls like little worker bees.

STEVEN. Now we're bees?

MELANIE. Just get the shot. Lights, camera, action!

(The students start talking louder and more animated. STEVEN films them and MELANIE directs him as they blend in with the students who don't seem to mind being filmed. MELANIE instructs STEVEN to follow a couple of students with the camera as they exit.)

(Note: Throughout the play MELANIE and STEVEN will be seen filming students during transitions. Sometimes the students will relate to them, other times they will just be ignored. These nonverbal appearances are up to you depending on your staging and production needs.)

Scene Two

(DANIELLE and ANNA remain on stage. DANIELLE spots ANNA and crosses to her.)

DANIELLE. What's up?
ANNA. Not much.
DANIELLE. Where's Lisa?
ANNA. Home sick.
DANIELLE. Wanna ditch?
ANNA. No way.
DANIELLE. You scared?
ANNA. You bet.
DANIELLE. How come?
ANNA. Mom's mad.
DANIELLE. Last night?
ANNA. That's right.
DANIELLE. Who told?
ANNA. My brother.
DANIELLE. Your brother?
ANNA. Saw me.
DANIELLE. What happened?
ANNA. I'm grounded.
DANIELLE. How long?
ANNA. Two weeks.
DANIELLE. Weekends, too?
ANNA. Of course.
DANIELLE. You sure?
ANNA. I'm positive.

(A bell is heard.)

DANIELLE. What class?
ANNA. English 2.
DANIELLE. Mrs. Green?
ANNA. Meany Greeny.

DANIELLE. Hard course?
ANNA. Not really.
DANIELLE. Talk later?
ANNA. Text me.

(ANNA exits. TAYLOR enters. DANIELLE crosses to her.)

DANIELLE. Wanna ditch?
TAYLOR. Right now?
DANIELLE. Best time.
TAYLOR. Good point.
DANIELLE. Let's go.

(They head off.)

Scene Three

(SCOTT enters and is immediately set upon by REESE. She looks around nervously as she pulls him to the side.)

REESE. You got the stuff?

SCOTT. Keep your voice down. Do you want to get busted or something?

REESE. Just give it to me.

SCOTT. You got the money?

(REESE pulls some cash out of her pocket. She looks around and slips it to SCOTT. He pulls a book out of his bag and hands it to her. REESE thumbs through it and is pleased with what she bought.)

Remember. If you're caught you didn't buy that from me.

(REESE exits.)

(to audience) What? You thought it was a drug deal? Please. Drugs are so last millennium. What I sell is much better. Textbooks. But not just any textbooks. These books were pre-owned by some of the smartest students in this school. Students that highlight the most important parts of what is being taught from those books. With lots of little hand written notes. You see, I figured out long ago that these are more valuable than gold. Most of the teachers here don't change their methods from year to year. The smart kids know what the most important things are that they teach. So I wait until the last day of class and make them an offer for their books before anyone else can. Then I sell them to kids the next year for double what I paid. They get a book that allows them to read only the important stuff and I get lots of easy cash. It's a win/win situation as they say.

(Another student approaches him and hands him some cash. SCOTT pulls out a book from his backpack and makes the deal.)

Business is so good, I'm thinking of opening a store on eBay. Then I can start bidding wars. The irony of this is that I only got a C in business class last semester. Probably would have done better if I hadn't sold valedictorian Eric Kelsey's business book and kept it for myself. I may not be the best student…but I'm going to make a killing in the real world. Grades are for amateurs, not entrepreneurs.

*(Another **STUDENT** approaches **SCOTT**.)*

What do you need?

STUDENT. Alegbra 2.

SCOTT. I got that.

STUDENT. Do you take Visa?

SCOTT. Let's talk.

(The two of them exit.)

Scene Four

(CHARLENE is standing in front of her locker typing something on her smartphone. SHELLY enters and runs over to her, giggling as she does.)

SHELLY. *(whispers excitedly)* Oh my God! Did you see how many comments we got?

CHARLENE. Yeah, I saw.

SHELLY. That thing has gone viral!

CHARLENE. 200 comments isn't viral.

SHELLY. I am so tempted to tell everyone we did it.

CHARLENE. I figured you would have already done that.

SHELLY. No way. We could get in major trouble. They're really cracking down on stuff like this.

CHARLENE. You mean cyberbullying.

SHELLY. I wouldn't call what we did bullying. It was a little joke, that's all.

CHARLENE. To us it's a joke, to Chaz it isn't. We posted some pretty bad lies about him.

SHELLY. Yeah, well it's not like Chaz the Spaz hasn't been made fun of by everybody else at this school.

CHARLENE. Not like this he hasn't.

SHELLY. Oh come on, it was funny. Besides, we did it at the *Cyber Cafe* under a fake name. They can't trace it back to us. They're not going to know we did it unless one of us tells and that isn't gonna happen.

(Long pause, SHELLY gets concerned.)

SHELLY. Oh my God… You're not thinking of saying something are you?

CHARLENE. Chaz isn't at school today.

SHELLY. What's that got to do with anything?

CHARLENE. He probably saw it. The way it was making the rounds how could he not.

SHELLY. What's your point?

CHARLENE. My point is…I started thinking about how I'd feel if someone posted mean lies about me and I became the joke of the school because of it.

SHELLY. He's used to it. He's been the joke of this school ever since I can remember.

CHARLENE. Well, we just dog piled on that big time. What if this pushes him over the edge? What if he does something stupid?

SHELLY. He wouldn't do that. *(pause)* Would he?

CHARLENE. I'm not going to take that chance. I deleted it.

SHELLY. What!?

CHARLENE. I deleted it from the page.

(SHELLY pulls out her cellphone and searches.)

SHELLY. Oh no…it's gone. *(angry)* You know, that also deleted all the comments!

CHARLENE. Uh…yeah…that's the point.

SHELLY. I can't believe you did that without asking me.

CHARLENE. We never should have put it up there.

SHELLY. Like I said, no one is going to catch us.

CHARLENE. I didn't take it down because I'm worried someone will catch us. I took it down because it's mean and we never should have done it.

SHELLY. You're being crazy. Let's talk about this…

CHARLENE. I can't. I'm going over to Chaz's house.

SHELLY. What? Why?

CHARLENE. To see if he's okay…and tell him I was the one that did it.

SHELLY. You are crazy.

CHARLENE. Don't worry; I'm going to tell him I did it alone. He'll never know you were in on it unless you tell him yourself.

SHELLY. Me?

CHARLENE. Yes, you.

SHELLY. No way.

CHARLENE. That's your call.

*(**CHARLENE** exits.)*

SHELLY. Charlene…

*(**SHELLY** thinks about following **CHARLENE**, but doesn't. She exits in the opposite direction.)*

Scene Five

(We hear dramatic Court-TV-like music. **TYLER** *takes the stage and announces* **MEGAN***'s entrance.)*

TYLER. This is Megan. She bought a new dress for what she thought was a very important date only to be stood up for that date. She is suing for $75.89...the cost of the dress.

(JUSTIN *enters as* **TYLER** *announces him.)*

TYLER. This is the defendant, Justin. He says he didn't make the date because his car broke down on the way to Megan's house and he had to walk back home. He was going to call her and explain what happened but she had left 15 messages on his cellphone and he wanted nothing more to do with this psycho girl. He's accused of pulling a disappearing act. He's filed a countersuit for $50 for harassment and mental duress. *(pause)* These two have decided to settle their case here in our forum, The Student's Court. And now, here's your Student Judge, the Honorable Amber Mackenzie.

(AMBER, *wearing a robe, enters and sits on either a high stool or two cubes.)*

AMBER. All right, I've read both of your statements. Megan, you are suing Justin for $75.89, the cost of a new dress you bought for a date with him. What happened?

MEGAN. Well, your honor, Justin had been following me around for weeks and acting all goofy and stuff so I knew he wanted to ask me out. Guys do that. So he finally gets up the courage and asks me to go to the movies.

AMBER. What movie were you going to see?

MEGAN. We were going to _____ *(Name any big movie currently playing at your local theater.)*

AMBER. I just saw that, it's so good!

MEGAN. Well, I wanted to see it but it didn't happen. Justin never showed up and I had bought a new dress and everything. I called him to find out why he stood me up and he never returned my calls.

AMBER. Do you have the dress here?

MEGAN. Yes, Megan…I mean, your honor.

(She holds up a dress.)

AMBER. I love it…that is so you!

MEGAN. Unfortunately, I never got to wear it because Justin blew me off…

(MEGAN starts to cry, but it's not very believable.)

AMBER. You poor thing. (*to* **JUSTIN**) All right, Jerkstin… What do you have to say for yourself?

JUSTIN. First of all I wasn't following her around and acting goofy. I've known Megan for years. I thought maybe she might be a fun date so I asked her out.

AMBER. Fun date? Yeah, whatever that means.

JUSTIN. So, anyway, I get in my car to go pick her up and get about halfway there and my timing belt broke and…

AMBER. Timing belt? Look, don't try to confuse the court with stupid guy car talk.

JUSTIN. Okay…uh…my car broke down. I walked back home and by the time I got there I found out she had left like all these threatening messages on my cell…

AMBER. Unbelievable. You have a cellphone and you didn't call her when your car broke down. Maybe she could have come and picked you up.

MEGAN. I would have.

JUSTIN. Well, that's the thing. I was running late and I forgot to take my cell with me.

MEGAN. You couldn't have used a pay phone?

AMBER. Yeah, what about a pay phone?

JUSTIN. What's a pay phone?

AMBER. There are still a few around. You know what I think, I think you changed your mind about the date with Megan and went out with someone else or watched some sort of stupid sports thing on TV or just plain forgot about it…but I'm not buying your car breaking down or your cellphone being left at home.

JUSTIN. But I have a receipt from Manny's Auto Repair that shows I had the timing belt replaced the next day.

AMBER. I don't care. I'm tired of guys like you treating women as if they were some kind of Kleenex that you can use and throw away. I find in favor of the Plaintiff for the amount of the dress and also awarding her the $50 you were countersuing for because I think she was the one who suffered, not you.

(AMBER bangs her gavel; crosses and gives a consoling hug to MEGAN and then exits.)

(JUSTIN crosses over to TYLER for follow-up.)

TYLER. The litigants are now leaving the courtroom. So Justin, how do you feel about the judge's ruling?

JUSTIN. It's totally wrong. She wouldn't even look at my receipt. It's obvious to me since she's Megan's friend that I didn't have a chance. And why do I have to pay for the dress…it's not like it was ruined or anything. She can still wear it. I'm going to appeal this injustice!

TYLER. Where?

JUSTIN. I'll take it all the way to the Supreme Court if I have to.

TYLER. *(sarcastic)* Yeah, well good luck with that. Are you ever going to ask Megan out again?

JUSTIN. Uh…well…maybe. I was thinking about asking her to the prom. But she's going to have to pick me up.

(JUSTIN exits. MEGAN crosses to TYLER.)

TYLER. So, Megan. The judge ruled in your favor. Do you feel vindicated?

MEGAN. What?

TYLER. Do you feel better now?

MEGAN. Totally. And I hope this sends a message out to all guys that you can't just stand us up on dates and get away with it.

TYLER. Would you ever go out with Justin if he asked you out again?

MEGAN. No way. *(quickly)* Why, did he say something?

TYLER. He said he might ask you to the prom.

MEGAN. Really? Well, uh...I'd have to think about it. I mean, I would! *(looking off)* Justin...Justin, wait up.

(MEGAN exits)

TYLER. So that brings to an end the case of the "stand up for justice." If you have a dispute, don't try to handle it yourself...settle it here in *The Student's Court.*

(Dramatic music fades up as TYLER exits.)

Scene Six

(NATE enters and looks around. He then addresses the audience.)

NATE. I was reading about these goats the other day. They're called myotonic goats otherwise known as "fainting goats." What happens to them is that when they panic their muscles freeze for about ten seconds or so and they fall over as if they have fainted. They even have some videos of them on YouTube. Now to most people that's kind of funny but to me it hits too close to home. No, I'm not a goat but when I panic I kind of seize up. I don't fall over but I just can't do anything. Can't move. Can't talk. Can't function. I don't panic often, but when I do…it's a big problem. That's why I have never been on a date with a girl. Oh, I've wanted to, but the few times I've tried I seized right up and couldn't ask them. I even tried calling the girl instead of a face to face confrontation because I thought it wouldn't cause me to panic so much. But as soon as I heard her voice nothing came out of me. They would just say, "Hello, hello, is anybody there?" and then hang up. It would take a full minute after that before I could get my voice to work. My mom took me to her shrink, Dr. Johansson, and he's been working with me. He said I need to practice what I'm going to say and visualize asking a particular girl out before doing so. That way I would be more confident and I wouldn't panic. So I've been practicing all week and the time has come. I'm going to ask Millicent out. She's in my English class and I think she kinda likes me, although I've never spoken to her. Her locker is right there and she always stops to switch books between second and third period. *(looks offstage)* There she is now…right on schedule.

(MILLICENT enters. NATE crosses to her confidently. He opens his mouth and…seizes up. His mouth is stuck in the open position and his eyes are the size of fried eggs. He

can only emit a few unintelligible grunts. **MILLICENT** *gives him a disapproving look and then exits.* **NATE** *follows after her, grunting – and even a couple of goat "baaahhhs" as he goes.)*

Scene Seven

(Four students enter the stage. They all wear varsity letter sweaters or jackets, but they are not athletes by any stretch of the imagination.)

MIKE. I'm Mike.

SHARON. Sharon.

BIANCA. Bianca.

ISAAC. Isaac.

MIKE. The Dork.

SHARON. The Brainbox.

BIANCA. The Misfit.

ISAAC. The Nerd.

MIKE. At least that's what we used to be called.

SHARON. Until we banded together and became a team.

BIANCA. And pooled our collective intelligence.

ISAAC. To compete in the newly formed State Scholastic Competition.

MIKE. Studying on weekends.

SHARON. Working our minds.

BIANCA. Busting our brains.

ISAAC. Each one an expert in their area of choice.

MIKE. Mathematics.

SHARON. Science.

BIANCA. The arts.

ISAAC. The world.

MIKE. And so we began our quest. Local competition?

ALL. We aced it.

SHARON. Regional competition?

ALL. We nailed it.

BIANCA. State competition?

ALL. They didn't stand a chance.

ISAAC. National competition?

ALL. We blew everyone away.

MIKE. We became instant celebrities.

SHARON. Overnight sensations.

BIANCA. Everyone wanted to know us.

ISAAC. We put this school on the map.

MIKE. And so we returned, we conquering heroes.

SHARON. To newfound fame.

BIANCA. To well earned respect.

ISAAC. To decorated lockers!

(They all look at him.)

ISAAC. Hey they used to shove me in my locker…now it's a shrine.

MIKE. What was the basketball team's record?

SHARON. 2 and 12

BIANCA. What was the football team's record?

ISAAC. 4 and 6

MIKE. What was our record?

ALL. 15 and 0.

MIKE. So give a cheer for us, you pom-pom bouncing cheerleaders.

SHARON. Polish up the awards.

BIANCA. Come to our victory parade.

ISAAC. And decorate our lockers!

MIKE. Because we are no longer…The Dork.

SHARON. The Brainbox.

BIANCA. The Misfit.

ISAAC. The Nerd.

BIG MIKE. We are Mike…

SHARON. Sharon…

BIANCA. Bianca…

ISAAC. And Isaac.

ALL. And we are the champions of the world!

(They four of them head off as other students enter. The students applaud them as they walk by.)

Scene Seven

(Four students enter the stage. They all wear varsity letter sweaters or jackets, but they are not athletes by any stretch of the imagination.)

MIKE. I'm Mike.

SHARON. Sharon.

BIANCA. Bianca.

ISAAC. Isaac.

MIKE. The Dork.

SHARON. The Brainbox.

BIANCA. The Misfit.

ISAAC. The Nerd.

MIKE. At least that's what we used to be called.

SHARON. Until we banded together and became a team.

BIANCA. And pooled our collective intelligence.

ISAAC. To compete in the newly formed State Scholastic Competition.

MIKE. Studying on weekends.

SHARON. Working our minds.

BIANCA. Busting our brains.

ISAAC. Each one an expert in their area of choice.

MIKE. Mathematics.

SHARON. Science.

BIANCA. The arts.

ISAAC. The world.

MIKE. And so we began our quest. Local competition?

ALL. We aced it.

SHARON. Regional competition?

ALL. We nailed it.

BIANCA. State competition?

ALL. They didn't stand a chance.

ISAAC. National competition?

ALL. We blew everyone away.

MIKE. We became instant celebrities.

SHARON. Overnight sensations.

BIANCA. Everyone wanted to know us.

ISAAC. We put this school on the map.

MIKE. And so we returned, we conquering heroes.

SHARON. To newfound fame.

BIANCA. To well earned respect.

ISAAC. To decorated lockers!

(They all look at him.)

ISAAC. Hey they used to shove me in my locker…now it's a shrine.

MIKE. What was the basketball team's record?

SHARON. 2 and 12

BIANCA. What was the football team's record?

ISAAC. 4 and 6

MIKE. What was our record?

ALL. 15 and 0.

MIKE. So give a cheer for us, you pom-pom bouncing cheerleaders.

SHARON. Polish up the awards.

BIANCA. Come to our victory parade.

ISAAC. And decorate our lockers!

MIKE. Because we are no longer…The Dork.

SHARON. The Brainbox.

BIANCA. The Misfit.

ISAAC. The Nerd.

BIG MIKE. We are Mike…

SHARON. Sharon…

BIANCA. Bianca…

ISAAC. And Isaac.

ALL. And we are the champions of the world!

(They four of them head off as other students enter. The students applaud them as they walk by.)

Scene Eight

(CHELSEA sits on a cube holding a yellow notepad. She writes something then rips the page off the pad, crumbles it up and tosses it to the floor next to other crumpled up papers.)

(RACHEL enters excitedly.)

CHELSEA. You're like an hour late. This thing is due today and I got nothin'.

RACHEL. Band practice ran long.

CHELSEA. Not my problem. Remember our deal…you help me write my story for English class and I hook you up with Brandon.

RACHEL. I know, I know. Taken care of.

(RACHEL pulls a few papers from her backpack.)

RACHEL. I found this in my Mom's closet.

CHELSEA. What's that?

RACHEL. A story she wrote in high school. She got an A plus on it. My mom's a great writer.

CHELSEA. Yeah? So…

RACHEL. So, we use the basic story and tweak it a little.

CHELSEA. Might work.

RACHEL. It's called "The Sweetheart Dance"…and it takes place at a high school dance.

CHELSEA. Sounds good so far. Tell me the story.

RACHEL. Well, it's the biggest dance of the year. Romantic music is playing.

(Lights dim a bit. We hear the sound of a slow song.)

RACHEL. Kids are dancing together, cheek to cheek.

CHELSEA. Cheek to cheek?

RACHEL. That's what they used to call dancing real close to each other.

(Several students appear and they start to dance…real close to each other.)

RACHEL. And the King and Queen have just been crowned. The King is Bart: handsome all-state quarterback.

*(A student playing **BART** enters. He wears a varsity letter jacket and a crown on his head.)*

RACHEL. The Queen is Annette…most popular girl in the school.

*(Another student playing **ANNETTE** enters; she also wears a crown. They start dancing together. **RACHEL** and **CHELSEA** watch them.)*

ANNETTE. Oh Bart isn't it great we were chosen King and Queen of the Sweetheart Dance. It's so perfect.

BART. Not as perfect as you are.

RACHEL. There's another girl at the dance: A plain-Jane type who wears glasses named…uh…Jane.

*(Another student playing **JANE** enters. She watches **BART** and **ANNETTE** dance with a sad and longing look on her face.)*

RACHEL. She's had a crush on Bart for years but she thinks he doesn't know she even exists. *(pause)* Come to think of it she looks a lot like my mom did in high school.

JANE. Hi Annette. *(dreamy)* Hi Bart.

ANNETTE. *(to **BART**)* Oh God. What is Jane doing here? This dance is for sweethearts not lonely hearts. Ha ha!

RACHEL. But here's the twist. Bart secretly has a thing for plain brainiac girls. He dumps Annette and asks Jane to dance.

*(**BART** tosses **ANNETTE** aside and crosses to **JANE**.)*

BART. Hey babe, may I have this dance? I love plain brainiac girls.

*(**BART** and **JANE** dance real close to each other.)*

CHELSEA. Then what?

RACHEL. They…uh…find true love and get married and stuff. Doesn't matter. Ms. Matthews will love it.

CHELSEA. I don't think so. The story seems really dated. From another era. Might have worked for your mom's generation but not now in 20__. *(Name the current year.)* I need to update it a bit.

(The music stops. **BART, JANE,** *and* **ANNETTE** *have stopped and are listening to* **CHELSEA** *and* **RACHEL.***)*

RACHEL. Update it how?

CHELSEA. I like the dance idea. But not the music they're playing. It needs something more current.

(The music changes to music from whatever is a top song right now.)

CHELSEA. Hate the football jersey. Jocks are so cliché. We'll make him more of a sensitive guy, but at the same time he's cold and mysterious in a vampire kind of way.

*(***BART** *takes off his football jersey and combs back his hair. Flashes a sensitive and seductive pouty look. He crosses to* **ANNETTE** *and they start to dance together again while* **JANE** *looks on.)*

CHELSEA. And this whole "he's hot for the plain girl" thing has been done a million times squared. I've got a better idea. Annette has a crush on Jane!

RACHEL. What?

CHELSEA. Yeah, she's gay and decides to use the dance to finally come out after years of keeping it a secret.

RACHEL. I don't think that's a good idea.

CHELSEA. It's genius. Ms. Matthews is too, so that's guaranteed to get me an "A" just for that.

RACHEL. Ms. Matthews is a lesbian? How come I didn't know that?

CHELSEA. Because it doesn't matter. Anyway, as I was saying…Annette dumps Bart and goes after what she really wants.

*(***ANNETTE** *tosses* **BART** *aside the same way* **BART** *had previously tossed her. She heads over to* **JANE.***)*

ANNETTE. Hey babe, may I have this dance? I love plain brainiac girls.

(*JANE is all for it.* **ANNETTE** *and* **JANE** *start to dance.*)

CHELSEA. Now we got something. Thanks, Rachel. I'll go make a copy of your mom's story and use it as a blueprint with my new changes.

(**CHELSEA** *exits.* **ANNETTE** *and* **JANE** *follow her off.*)

(**RACHEL** *notices* **BART** *is still there and crosses over to him.*)

RACHEL. I know…I know. I'm as confused as you are.

(**BART** *doesn't know what to do, so he says his written line.*)

BART. Uh… Hey babe, may I have this dance?

RACHEL. No, but I'd love some Starbucks. Come on, I'll buy you a latte…and try to explain this new world to you. That's if I can figure it out for myself.

(*She takes his hand and leads him offstage.*)

BART. (*as they exit*) What's a Starbucks?

Scene Nine

*(Several girls, including **BEVERLY**, are in the girls' restroom, putting on makeup and fixing their hair. Suddenly we see several **BOYS** push a rolling desk chair into the restroom and then run away. Sitting on the desk chair and wrapped in toilet paper, is **GILBERT**. His mouth has duct tape over it, and duct tape is also wrapped around his chest, attaching him to the chair. There is a mix of laughter and disgust as the Girls all react to him and exit the bathroom. **BEVERLY** stays behind.)*

BEVERLY. Let me guess…boys' bathroom was full?

GILBERT. Mmmmm…fftt…

*(**BEVERLY** crosses to him and removes the duct tape from his mouth. **GILBERT** yelps from the tape being ripped away.)*

BEVERLY. You could get in a lot of trouble for being in here.

GILBERT. Not here by choice.

BEVERLY. I know you…you're in the band. Tuba, right?

GILBERT. Yeah, my parents idea, not mine. Not the Tuba… that was Mr. Geisler's idea. Said I had the lungs for it. Personally, I wanted to learn to play the guitar but the band doesn't have one of those so I got stuck with whatever they needed.

BEVERLY. Yeah, well…

*(She starts to leave. **GILBERT** struggles a bit, bound by the tape which restrains him.)*

GILBERT. Wait a minute. You're not going to leave me here are you?

BEVERLY. Serves you right.

GILBERT. Serves me right? I didn't do anything.

BEVERLY. You're in the girls' bathroom…that's something.

GILBERT. Like I said, not by choice. Those guys threw me in here.

BEVERLY. You must have done something to earn that.

GILBERT. Yeah, I dared to walk in their hallway…and not be a jock.

BEVERLY. That's it.

GILBERT. Well, that and let the air out of Larry Edison's tires.

BEVERLY. Do you have a death wish? He's twice your size.

GILBERT. He's also a tormenter.

BEVERLY. Yeah, I know. So he picked on you…that's life.

GILBERT. I'm used to it. I deal with it. Mostly with my mouth which gets me in a lot of trouble but my motto is…if you're not fit, develop your wit. I'm pretty good with comebacks when people mock me.

BEVERLY. Good for you. So, you mouthed off and let the air out of his tires?

GILBERT. No, I let the air out of his tires because he picked on someone who isn't real good at standing up for himself. A kid in the band and we have to look out for our bandmates. Jeremiah didn't do anything to deserve abuse from a cretin like Larry.

BEVERLY. Jeremiah?

GILBERT. Yeah, he's a freshman. Plays the trombone…

BEVERLY. Jeremiah Colson?

GILBERT. You know him?

BEVERLY. He's my cousin.

GILBERT. Really? Man…you guys don't look anything alike. He's so small and frail and you're…like really good looking and stuff.

BEVERLY. We're cousins, not twins. Jeremiah's a great kid. He's just shy. And hasn't really come into his own yet.

GILBERT. Yeah, I agree…he's a good kid.

BEVERLY. So Larry was picking on him?

GILBERT. Smacked him around and then grabbed his backpack. Real mature, huh?

BEVERLY. So how did you get involved?

GILBERT. I grabbed the backpack, said something about Larry's block shaped head and then returned it to Jeremiah before I took off running. Larry caught me and slapped me up one side and down the other. It was a real slapfest. Since slapping back wouldn't do much good I did the next best thing…I hatched a plan to let the air out of the muscle head's muscle car.

BEVERLY. Pretty sneaky.

GILBERT. Yup. Would have been the perfect crime…well that is if he hadn't caught me in the act. He threatened to call the police so I used my mom's Triple-A card and they came out and filled up his tire. I thought that was the end of it until today…and that's how I landed in here. Big fun, eh?

BEVERLY. You know what you are?

GILBERT. A loser?

BEVERLY. No…you're a hero.

(**BEVERLY** *thinks for a minute and opens up her purse.*)

GILBERT. Hey, don't even think about giving me a reward. I did it…

(*She gives him a look and holds up a nail file.*)

GILBERT. You're going to do my nails?

(**BEVERLY** *rolls her eyes and crosses behind* **GILBERT**. *She uses the nail file to cut through the duct tape that holds him. He is free from the duct tape. He stands up and stretches a bit.*)

BEVERLY. That's for looking out for my cousin.

GILBERT. Thanks.

BEVERLY. Don't know many guys that would put themselves in danger like that to help someone less fortunate.

GILBERT. I don't really consider Jeremiah less fortunate. He's got more going for him than most kids.

BEVERLY. Yeah he does. And he's lucky to have a friend like you.

(BEVERLY starts to leave.)

GILBERT. Uh, Beverly…wait…

BEVERLY. What?

GILBERT. Well…I…uh…was wondering…. Would you do me a favor?

BEVERLY. Depends.

GILBERT. Well, you see…I know that Larry and some other guys are probably waiting for me to come out of here and be all embarrassed and stuff. And I don't want to give them that satisfaction. I was wondering if you'd…

BEVERLY. You want me to tell them off?

GILBERT. No, no, no…nothing like that. Something much better. Well if they saw you and I walk out together… uh…this is awkward…but if you and I would be holding hands it would really mess with their heads. Now, I realize what that would do to your reputation and I would make sure no one would think we were dating or anything.

BEVERLY. I'd be glad to. And I don't really care what anybody thinks. But I do have one condition.

GILBERT. Anything.

BEVERLY. Take off the toilet paper before we leave.

GILBERT. Oh…yeah…right.

(GILBERT unwraps the toilet paper quickly. When it's off, BEVERLY holds out her hand and GILBERT takes it. They exit together.)

Scene Ten

(**DYLAN** *hobbles in on crutches. He wears a football jersey.*)

DYLAN. When my dad went to high school he was a star quarterback. But the apple in this case fell about as far from the tree as it possibly could. Yeah, I'm on the team but just one step above the mascot. You see the team is divided into squads: There's the first string, second string, buzzard squad, crow-bait squad and then me, Dylan. That's right, I'm my own squad. I'm the guy the coach puts in when we're ahead by 50 or behind by so much it doesn't matter. So far this season I've played exactly 39 seconds. My parents come to every game and I'm not sure who's more embarrassed – my dad or me. He doesn't say anything after the games and that hurts more than if he would actually yell at me for being such a loser. My mom probably warns him not to, but I can see in his face that he's disappointed and doesn't understand why I don't have his mad football skills. *(motions to crutches)* Oh, these? Fortunately I racked up my knee pretty bad at the game last Friday. Well, not *in* the game…a guy from the other team ran into me on the sidelines after he caught a pass. Doctor said no more football. Greatest thing that ever happened to me. Now I can finally do what I want to do…start a rock band! I got a great voice and natural musical talent. Just like my mom. You know, genetics are a funny thing. Like spinning a big roulette wheel. You never know just what number it's going to land on. Went right past the sports gene and stopped on "rock star." Don't be too hard on yourself, dad. Yeah, mom's DNA was more dominant than yours, but I'm still proud of you anyway.

(**DYLAN** *hobbles off, singing a current hit song as he goes.*)

Scene Eleven

(EMILY spots MARCUS who is talking to another BOY. She crosses to him.)

EMILY. You got a minute.

(MARCUS seems annoyed and bids good-bye to the BOY he was talking to.)

MARCUS. Make it fast.

EMILY. What's your hurry? It's your lunch period.

MARCUS. And I'd like to enjoy it. Besides, talking to my sister is not good for my rep.

EMILY. You don't have a rep. Listen, this is important. It's about mom and dad.

MARCUS. Oh, so all of a sudden you care about mom again.

EMILY. What's that supposed to mean?

MARCUS. Since you moved over to Dad's place you hardly talk to her anymore.

EMILY. We've been through this a million times. I didn't move in with him… I'm just staying there to help him through the transition. It's the first time he's living alone in a long time.

MARCUS. That's his fault.

EMILY. So how is mom doing?

MARCUS. She has good days and bad.

EMILY. You know they still love each other.

MARCUS. Yeah, right.

EMILY. I caught dad looking at their wedding video the other day.

MARCUS. Probably trying to remember which bridesmaid he hit on.

EMILY. Come on, give him a break.

MARCUS. He cheated on mom. He doesn't deserve a break.

EMILY. And he's paid a terrible price for that. *(beat)* Look, I don't want to talk to you about that. It happened, it's over.

MARCUS. Then what do you want?

EMILY. I want you to help me with a scam.

MARCUS. Scam? Okay, not you got my interest. You know my theme song – "dirty deeds done dirt cheap!"

EMILY. It's not really a dirty deed. It's more like a surprise.

MARCUS. I don't like where this is going.

EMILY. I need you to help me to get mom and dad together in the same place this Saturday.

MARCUS. What?

EMILY. It's their anniversary.

MARCUS. They're not married anymore.

EMILY. Technically they still are. The divorce isn't final. And an anniversary is an anniversary no matter what because it happened in the past. So I came up with this idea that if you and I got them together at their favorite restaurant…they'd be stuck talking to each other.

MARCUS. Are you crazy?

EMILY. Maybe, but it's worth a try. I know they're still in love. If they could just talk it out. I know it's a long shot, but I know you want that to happen, too.

MARCUS. Dad was really watching their wedding video?

EMILY. More than once.

MARCUS. I don't know.

EMILY. If all else fails I've got a secret weapon.

MARCUS. Handcuffs?

EMILY. Something better.

*(She pulls something from her backpack, hands it to **MARCUS**.)*

MARCUS. What's this?

EMILY. Mom's yearbook from high school. I found it last week in the garage when I picked up my rollerblades. Check this out.

(opens up the yearbook)

EMILY. They always told us they dated in high school. Well, they were more serious than we thought. Read what dad wrote to her.

(**EMILY** *points to something written in it.*)

MARCUS. *(reads)* "To Muffin…" Muffin?

EMILY. That's what he used to call her.

MARCUS. "You are my one and only love. My heart will never be for another. I promise that I will love you forever and beyond. Daniel"

EMILY. Okay, so he was no poet. But he has forgotten about his promise. And I plan on reminding him of it.

MARCUS. Well, in order for your idea to even have a chance we have to come up with a good reason to get them both at the restaurant at the same time.

EMILY. That's where you come in. If anyone can make that happen, you can. I'll pay for their dinner if you find a way to get them there.

MARCUS. Maybe you should hire a referee, too.

EMILY. I don't think they'll need it. We're going to be a family again. I just know it.

(**MARCUS** *thinks for a moment; looks back at the yearbook.*)

MARCUS. Okay…I'm in.

EMILY. You're the best!

(*She hugs him. He pulls away when he sees a couple of* **GIRLS** *walk past them and stand talking nearby.*)

MARCUS. *(through clenched teeth)* What are you doing? We're at school, Emily!

EMILY. Right, right. Your rep. I'm sorry.

MARCUS. *(whispers)* I'll call you later.

(**EMILY** *exits excitedly.* **MARCUS** *tries to act cool as he addresses the* **GIRLS** *that have stopped talking and now look over at him.*)

MARCUS. 'Sup ladies.

Scene Twelve

(**MARISA** *storms onto the stage. She holds a few papers in her hand.*)

I am like so freakin' angry. Like I spent all night workin' on my book report for Mr. Melman's class and he like totally dissed me! *(looking at paper)* C minus? Really? It's a great report. Like I wasted my whole night on this when I coulda been over at Gina's house watchin' a movie. So I tell Mr. Melman, "Like what's your problem?" And he was all like "It's poorly written" and I was like "What? Are you like serious?" and he was all like "If you rewrite it I'll consider changing your grade if it's better." Oh my God! Are you like kidding me? It's like totally great right now. Let me read you the first paragraphic and you tell me I'm wrong. *(reads)* "The book was about this boy who like everyone thought was severely insane in the brain and he was all like buggin' about his parents. I like totally saw his point because my parents are rollin' up on me like every day. Jeremy was like so bored with his life he could gag and stuff and I like so relate to him for real deal!" *(to audience)* Now I ask you, is that like not great writing or what? I know, right? So, I decided I'm going to like go right over Melman's head with this and talk to the Principal. He'll see how I was like so wronged with this and rule on my half. He'll make Melman like totally give me the A that I like deserve. And I am like so proud of myself for standing up for myself and like not putting up with this injustice stuff for myself. You know what I think is goin' on here? I'm like being disseminated against because I'm like a free range thinker!

(**MARISA** *storms off.*)

Scene Thirteen

(VICTORIA, JANINE, and ERICA enter. They are in mid conversation...)

VICTORIA. It just doesn't make any sense.

JANINE. Makes perfect sense to me...it's one less class to worry about.

ERICA. Yeah, my parents will finally see an A on my report card.

VICTORIA. So you're going to give yourself an A?

JANINE. Well, duh? I sure don't plan on giving myself a D.

(ERICA and JANINE laugh.)

VICTORIA. Even if you didn't earn an A?

JANINE. Stop with the negativity, Victoria...and count your blessings. I just hope every teacher follows what Mr. Richards is doing.

ERICA. No way is that going to happen. I've never heard of a teacher telling students to pick the grade they feel they deserve. Do you think there's a catch?

JANINE. Maybe with another teacher, but not Richards. He's so proud of being this Zen kinda guy. He meant it. We get to tell him what grade we think we should get for his class...and that's the grade he's going to give us.

ERICA. This is like so great.

VICTORIA. I do think there's a catch.

JANINE. Stop.

VICTORIA. No, I mean he'll give you the grade and everything, but by making us tell him what we think we should get it puts pressure on us to be honest.

ERICA. What?

VICTORIA. I just can't say I deserve an A if I don't really deserve it.

JANINE. Why not?

VICTORIA. Because it wouldn't be right.

JANINE. There's nothing right about the grading system to begin with. It's always up to what they think we should get. It's just their opinion based on no real facts. Like last week when I got a B- on my science project. I spent all weekend on it. I "deserved" much better than the grade I got.

ERICA. Yeah, what she said.

VICTORIA. Maybe you did…but if you don't deserve a good grade in Richards' class then you shouldn't lie about it.

JANINE. Won't be a lie. I go to the class every day…I listen to him. What more does he want?

ERICA. Yeah, what more does he want?

VICTORIA. It's not about him, it's about us. Learning to be honest with ourselves. Not relying on others to tell us what we're worth.

JANINE. You're right…and I think I'm worth an A.

ERICA. Me, too.

JANINE. Hey, let's celebrate our good grades. Party at my house tonight. Movies, music, and more!

ERICA. I'm in!

VICTORIA. I'm not in. I'm going to study.

JANINE. He really messed your head up, didn't he? So just tell him you deserve a C and then you won't have to feel guilty.

ERICA. There you go.

(A bell is heard and they all exit offstage..)

Scene Fourteen

(**KIMBERLY** *enters and looks around to make sure she isn't being followed.*)

KIMBERLY. I have to be careful...I just got my allowance and my parents gave it to me in cash. If others were to find out I would surely get robbed of my great wealth. How much do I get for my allowance you are wondering? Well, my generous parents have bestowed upon me the titanic sum of...wait for it...five dollars! *(She pulls a $5 bill from her pocket)* How about that? Gee, what should I do with this fortune? Invest in the volatile stock market? Too risky. How about buying up real estate? No, the housing market is soft. I know, I could put it in the bank and live off the interest. *(angry)* Five dollars? For the whole week? Welcome to my nightmare, ladies and gentlemen. What century do my parents think I'm living in? Five dollars? How am I supposed to survive on this? If I want to go anywhere for fun it will have to be to the park and feed the pigeons with day old bread. And I will have to walk there because as far as I know they don't sell gasoline by the ounce. Forget about going to a movie. I can't even afford the popcorn. Five dollars? And what do I have to do to earn this paltry piece of green paper? Do the laundry, cook dinner, wash the car, babysit my little brother and a dozen other things that are too embarrassing to mention. The way I figure it, I'm making about ten cents an hour. These are sweatshop wages! Five dollars? Are you kidding me? My dad says he would give me more but he wants me to learn the value of money. Hey, dad, I got an "A" in business class. I know the value of money. But obviously you don't. Because if you did you'd realize that with the current rate of inflation and the dismal economic environment, this five dollar bill isn't worth the paper it's printed on. Five dollars? That does it. Tonight is the night I have a real serious talk with my parents. I am going to tell them the bitter truth…that as a teenager, I am definitely living below the poverty level. If things don't change for me I am going to vote my parents out of office! Five dollars? Seriously?

(She exits.)

Scene Fifteen

(**ALLY** *is talking with* **KITTY**. *Well, mostly* **KITTY** *talks.*)

KITTY. So I told her if she didn't stop coming looking over at my test I was going to tell Mr. Morrison that she...

(*She stops when she spots* **JEFF** *who has entered and is immediately set upon by several other students who ask him for his autograph.*)

KITTY. Oh my God, oh my God! Jeff's here...

(**KITTY** *runs over to him and joins the other students who excitedly react to getting an autograph.* **JEFF** *looks over at* **ALLY** *who has not joined the group and waves. He finishes signing and crosses over to her.*)

JEFF. Hi Ally.

ALLY. Looks like you got some major fans here.

JEFF. Yeah, well...wow, this is so weird being back here. I mean it seems like years since I've been here even though it's only been a few months.

ALLY. Your mom told me you were coming by today to clear out your locker.

JEFF. Yeah...I figured someone else could use the space. Gonna hate giving up the prime location. Took me three years to get it.

ALLY. Why are you really here, Jeff?

JEFF. Like I said, to clean out my locker.

ALLY. Come on. You don't need that stuff anymore. And you could have gotten someone else to do that for you. You're here to suck up all the love now that you're a big star.

JEFF. That's not it at all.

ALLY. It's okay. I'd probably do the same thing. Most of these kids ignored you when you went here and now they're all over you. Pretty good revenge if you ask me.

JEFF. I've been very lucky.

ALLY. More than luck. You were the best thing on that show. You deserved to win. The judges got it right. And I read that it was the highest rated finals ever for a TV talent show.

JEFF. Oh, thanks…but it still had a lot to do with luck.

ALLY. Things have really changed for you.

JEFF. Yeah, it's been crazy.

ALLY. Thanks for the necklace. But you shouldn't have. Way too much.

JEFF. I felt bad about missing your birthday. I really wanted to be there… but they put us all on that tour right away and then I was in the studio recording…

ALLY. Don't worry about it. I'm very happy for your success.

JEFF. I don't know. It's exciting and everything, but it's all happening so fast I haven't been able to process it yet.

(There is a long awkward pause.)

JEFF. I really miss you, Ally.

ALLY. Look, I better get to class…

(She starts out.)

JEFF. Wait. Just a couple of minutes.

(She stops.)

JEFF. Ally, you're right. I didn't come back here to clean out my locker.

ALLY. I know. It's okay. Like I said, I'd do the same thing.

JEFF. I didn't come back for that either. To tell you the truth I'm tired of the whole star thing and it's only been a few months. I suppose I should enjoy it while it lasts but I miss just being a nobody. I know that sounds weird, but I do. And I miss being with you.

ALLY. Well, not that much. I read in People magazine you're dating Jessica O'Brian.

JEFF. I went out with her a couple of times, but we're not dating. She is so in love with herself that she really doesn't need a date.

ALLY. She's gorgeous.

JEFF. And she knows it. *(pause)* Ally, I want you back in my life. I need you.

ALLY. You need me?

JEFF. I need us. More than ever before. I need someone who just knows me as plain old Jeff. You understand me. You know me…the good stuff and all my flaws. I've met a lot of girls like Jessica, but none of them are half as good as you.

ALLY. Wow, didn't expect this. I'd love for us to be together again. But that's kind of hard. I mean, you don't even go here anymore.

JEFF. I know. But I will make time. You're going to graduate this year… and when you do we can make this work.

ALLY. I'll be going to college next year.

JEFF. All right, well…I'll go there, too.

ALLY. No way. You're no college boy. Besides, you need to pursue your career. You've got talent and an opportunity that few ever get.

JEFF. You see, that's why I know you're the real deal. You think of others before you think of yourself.

(He kisses her. She wasn't expecting that, but is glad he did.)

ALLY. We'll talk later. I really need to go to class.

JEFF. Okay. But know one thing. I am going make this work. Whatever it takes.

*(**ALLY** starts to head off, then stops.)*

ALLY. You know something…I've gone to this school for twelve years now and never once skipped out. I think I've earned an afternoon off, don't you think?

JEFF. Like they say, being bad never felt so good. Come on, let's get out of here. Ever ride in a Ferrari?

ALLY. You have a Ferrari?

JEFF. No, I got my mom's Volvo. Just wanted to know if you ever rode in one.

*(**ALLY** playfully slaps him and they exit.)*

Scene Sixteen

*(We see **CANDACE** onstage and she reacts to the entrance of **REBECCA**, who is dressed in a cheerleader's outfit. Trailing **REBECCA**, are several boys who make up her entourage of worshippers. They all walk in front of **CANDACE** who glares at them. When they get to the opposite side of the stage they will freeze. **CANDACE** crosses downstage center and pulls out a large picture book from her backpack. She reads to the audience...)*

CANDACE. Once upon a time, in a high school not so far away, lived an evil Princess named *(looking over at **REBECCA**)* Rebecca. Oh, most of the villagers didn't think she was evil and worshipped her because they thought she was so perfect. She had everything – good looks, popularity, rich parents, and a phony smile that she would flash whenever she wanted to get her way. Also in the village, lived a kind and beautiful maiden, named *(referring to herself)* Candace. Now, no one seemed to realize that Candace was the real deal because she didn't go around flaunting herself, nor was she given everything in life. Candace had to work hard for the few crumbs of success that she had. She couldn't afford the best clothes, she didn't have teachers that gave her easy grades, and she didn't become a cheerleader even though her audition to become one was ten times better than Princess Rebecca's! But, Candace wasn't bitter. Because Candace knew that nothing lasts forever. As a matter of fact she knew that after high school ended the evil Princess Rebecca would have a hard time in life. She would not have the smarts to get in a good college, the work ethic to have a career, or the sustainable looks to have boys flock around her for very long. Candace also understood that life is so much more than the concrete and linoleum of this high school where shallowness and mediocrity reign supreme. Candace knew that once free from the spell and shadow of the evil Princess she would emerge into a world that would see her as the beautiful and smart true Princess that she really is. And in that real world she would find true love with the most handsome Prince in all the land. Candace would become the most sought after of them all and someday become Queen of Everything. And in just one more year she would start her own wonderful fairy tale. Candace would then live happily ever after. Evil Princess Rebecca...not so much.

(She closes the book and **REBECCA** *and her entourage unfreeze. They cross back in front of* **CANDACE**, *who scowls at them for a moment and then exits.)*

Scene Seventeen

(**MELANIE** *enters and spots* **STEVEN** *who turns and starts to head the other way to avoid her.*)

MELANIE. Steven, wait up…

(*He stops, knowing that he has been caught.*)

MELANIE. Where's your camera? I thought we agreed that you would have it with you at all times.

STEVEN. "We" didn't agree to that. "You" gave it to me as an order.

MELANIE. It was not an order…just a strong suggestion.

STEVEN. I need a couple days off. Besides, I have over 100 hours of footage already and it's only halfway through the school year.

MELANIE. Well, edit as you go…so you don't have to wait until the last minute.

STEVEN. I have been. And I have to admit there's some great stuff in there.

MELANIE. You see! Now it's okay if you take a few days off from filming this week because I need you to work overtime Saturday at the dance.

STEVEN. I wasn't planning on going.

MELANIE. No, I need you there. Especially to film the parking lot when everyone's making out. We need to put more sexy stuff in the video …it will help sales.

STEVEN. I really don't want to go.

MELANIE. What? You and Amelia are like Mr. and Mrs. GoToEveryDance.

STEVEN. Not anymore. She dumped me yesterday.

MELANIE. Ouch, sorry to hear that. (*upbeat*) But that will give you more time at the dance to get some great footage.

STEVEN. The reason she dumped me is because she's been seeing Brian Middleton. She'll be at the dance with him and I really don't want to deal with that.

MELANIE. That blows.

STEVEN. So if you want to get some great footage you'll have to shoot it yourself.

(**STEVEN** *starts to head off.* **MELANIE** *has to think quickly.*)

MELANIE. Revenge?

STEVEN. What?

(She scurries to him.)

MELANIE. This is perfect. You can shoot lots of footage of the two of them.

STEVEN. Why would I want to do that?

MELANIE. Because it would boost sales of our video yearbook if it had a big emotional onscreen breakup on it.

STEVEN. We already had that yesterday.

MELANIE. Not you. Brian and Amelia.

STEVEN. Never happen.

MELANIE. Maybe not on its own. But what if when Brian goes to the restroom I have my BFF Bonnie, aka The Hottest Girl in the School, accidentally on purpose run into him in the hall and seduce him. You of course will be tipped off so you can capture his complete submission to her on film. And I'll make sure someone tips Amelia off so she catches them in the act. High drama, baby!

STEVEN. You mean staging something to cause the breakup? I thought you wanted this video to be about the spontaneous reality of our school year.

MELANIE. And just like reality shows on TV...we plan the spontaneity.

STEVEN. So you want to take advantage of my breakup and need for revenge as a marketing tool for our project?

MELANIE. In a word, yes.

STEVEN. Okay…I'm in.

(STEVEN flashes an evil grin and then heads off.)

MELANIE. Ba-bam! I am good.

(MELANIE exits.)

Scene Eighteen

(MICHAEL enters. He sees ABIGAIL, turns quickly and walks the other way. Too late.)

ABIGAIL. Michael…you stop right there.

(He stops. She approaches him and we see she is carrying a doll that is about the same size as a baby.)

ABIGAIL. You've been avoiding us all day.

MICHAEL. Us?

ABIGAIL. Me and Little Nicky.

MICHAEL. I haven't been avoiding you.

ABIGAIL. I know you and I had a fight last night but don't take it out on our child.

MICHAEL. Don't start with that again.

ABIGAIL. He may be just a baby but he has feelings.

MICHAEL. You're delusional.

(ABIGAIL covers the doll's ears.)

ABIGAIL. Don't raise your voice to me in front of Little Nicky.

MICHAEL. That's enough, Abigail. I'm tired of this stupid game.

ABIGAIL. It's not a game! It's an assignment…and you are flunking out as a father.

MICHAEL. I'm not a father. And that's not a baby…it's a doll.

ABIGAIL. Michael!

MICHAEL. I don't care if Mrs. Oliver gives me an F…I'm done with this and I'm done with you.

ABIGAIL. You want a divorce?

MICHAEL. We're not married!

ABIGAIL. Little Nicky thinks we are. We're the only parents he knows.

MICHAEL. He's made out of rubber. His parents are a couple of workers who put him together in China.

ABIGAIL. I can't believe you're saying that.

MICHAEL. I can't believe you think that thing is real.

ABIGAIL. Don't call him a thing!

MICHAEL. It's a stupid doll, Abigail.

(**ABIGAIL** *starts to cry.*)

ABIGAIL. I can't believe this is happening.

MICHAEL. Nothing is happening. Man, I knew I never shoulda paired up with you to do this. I shoulda been with Melissa…

ABIGAIL. Melissa? She shoved her baby in her locker and doesn't even carry it around like we're supposed to.

MICHAEL. She realizes what you obviously don't…that this thing is a joke. We're only sixteen…we're too young to be parents.

ABIGAIL. This is supposed to help us prepare for when we are parents. And it has…I care for Little Nicky more than I've ever cared for anyone.

MICHAEL. Well big props to you…I don't see it that way. I don't want to be a father…now or ever.

ABIGAIL. What are you saying?

MICHAEL. I'm saying that I don't need to learn no stinkin' "parenting skills" because I don't ever want kids.

ABIGAIL. You can't be serious.

MICHAEL. I'm just like my Uncle Brad…he's 38 and never been married…and he says he never wants to.

ABIGAIL. You know what they call a man who's over 30 and still single?

MICHAEL. Yeah, they call him lucky!

(**MICHAEL** *starts to leave.*)

ABIGAIL. Where are you going?

MICHAEL. Anywhere but here.

ABIGAIL. What about your bonding time with Little Nicky?

MICHAEL. With any luck the only person I will be bonding with is Melissa tonight in the back seat of my car.

(*He exits.*)

ABIGAIL. Michael! *(to doll)* Don't you worry, Little Nicky… mommy will never abandon you like your heartless daddy.

(NATASHA enters and sees ABIGAIL.)

NATASHA. Hey, Abigail…Sandra and I are going to the mall. Wanna come?

ABIGAIL. Can't. I have to go find a lawyer.

NATASHA. A lawyer?

ABIGAIL. I'm getting a divorce…and I'll tell you this…he is going to pay child support or I'll have his deadbeat butt thrown in jail.

*(**ABIGAIL** storms off, leaving a confused **NATASHA** behind.)*

Scene Nineteen

*(**GINA** and **DANICA** sit quietly. Other students sit nearby.)*

GINA. You know what I hate about this library?

DANICA. Too many books, not enough magazines?

GINA. The quiet.

DANICA. All libraries are quiet.

GINA. Well, it's not right.

DANICA. What's not right about it?

GINA. It's like a strait-jacket.

DANICA. It's so people can think about what they're reading.

GINA. Most of the kids here think best when music is blasting and the TV is on.

DANICA. I guess you're right.

GINA. They only keep us quiet because of control.

DANICA. Control?

GINA. It's a conspiracy. Just one more way of keepin' us down.

DANICA. Down from what?

GINA. From whatever our free minds want to do.

DANICA. And what does your free mind want to do?

GINA. *(raises voice)* Scream out against injustice.

STUDENT. Ssshhhh.

DANICA. Keep it down…the Librarian is giving you the eye.

GINA. She's always givin' me the eye. She's in on it, you know.

DANICA. The conspiracy?

GINA. Yup.

DANICA. What are you so worked up about today?

*(**GINA** holds up a magazine.)*

GINA. I'm reading this article about how students have become so lazy that we don't care about anything anymore. We're kept in here like yolks in a big egg. The shell shields us from all the terrible things in the world and we become numb to reality. We've all become like sheep. Even though the world is falling apart, we just sit in front of the TV or computer screen and pretend that everything is all right.

DANICA. You watch more TV than anybody I know.

GINA. Well, maybe I shouldn't.

DANICA. So what are you gonna do about it?

GINA. Maybe I'll just stand up on top of my chair right here, right now, and protest the silence.

DANICA. Protest the silence?

GINA. By screaming out loud.

DANICA. What good is that going to do?

GINA. It would let people know that I care.

DANICA. The only thing it would let people know…is that you're insane.

GINA. Well, I'm gonna do it.

DANICA. When?

GINA. Soon.

DANICA. Well let me know right before you do so I can get away from you.

(**GINA** *looks around for a moment.*)

GINA. It's time for this caterpillar to shed her cocoon.

DANICA. Your scream won't change the world, Gina. It will just make everyone laugh at you.

GINA. They laughed at Einstein, too.

DANICA. Only when he screamed out loud in a library.

GINA. A movement of many starts but with one voice.

DANICA. I know you didn't make that up…

GINA. No, I saw it on a box of herb tea, but it really got me thinking.

DANICA. In your case thinking is a dangerous thing.

GINA. This is no game…this is my destiny.

(GINA stands up on her cube.)

DANICA. Oh no…

GINA. WAKE UP PEOPLE…RAGE AGAINST THE SILENCE RAGE AGAINST INJUSTICE!

(DANICA cringes. The other students look at GINA for a moment as she smiles in victory, but then they go back to their reading as if nothing has happened. GINA climbs back down and sits.)

GINA. The movement has begun!

DANICA. The only movement I see is the librarian coming this way.

(GINA looks. She gets up and makes a quick exit.)

Scene Twenty

(VINCENT enters holding a report card.)

VINCENT. In my hand I hold perhaps the worst report card of my entire life. But am I nervous? No. Am I afraid of the consequences? Not in the least. Do I worry about impending doom because of this? Not gonna happen. Why? Because despite the letters on this report card, I am incredibly smart. Smart enough to do a little research to prepare for the fight I will have with my parents when they see it. When they start to criticize me I will unleash some factoids that will silence them forever. *(as if talking to his parents)* "Well, Mom and Dad did you know that Albert Einstein didn't speak until he was four years old or read until he was seven. Walt Disney was fired from a newspaper because he was told that he lacked imagination and had no good ideas. Bill Gates dropped out of college and his first business was a bust. Thomas Edison made over a thousand failed attempts before inventing a light bulb that worked. Oprah Winfrey was fired as a TV reporter. Vincent Van Gogh sold only one painting in his life and that was to a friend for very little money. Steven Spielberg was rejected from film school three times. And Michael Jordan was cut from his high school basketball team. So, Mother and Father do not look at my report card as a measure of my potential. If anything, these bad grades are a good thing. You should be proud. Because this is proof positive that I am greatness in training like all those famous people. And I am well on my way to becoming the success that you so desperately want me to be. Celebrate your son and reward this temporary failure!"

(VINCENT looks proudly at his report card and then exits.)

Scene Twenty-One

(BIG STEVE enters stage right and sees MIRANDA enter stage left. They meet in the middle, glaring at each other in a threatening manner for a moment before speaking.)

BIG STEVE. Bet no one's asked you to the prom yet.

MIRANDA. Bet every girl in this school's turned you down.

(They stare at each other with contempt for a moment.)

BIG STEVE. So you want to go together.

MIRANDA. Yeah, okay.

BIG STEVE. *(snarling)* I'll pick you up at 7.

MIRANDA. Yeah fine.

*(They sneer at each other and **BIG STEVE** exits stage left; **MIRANDA** exits stage right.)*

Scene Twenty-Two

(**THOMAS**, *wearing shorts and tank top, hides behind a couple of cubes, looking up to see if the coast is clear. Ducks back down when a couple of other boys walk from stage left to stage right. One of the boys,* **RANDALL**, *stays behind as the other one exits.*)

RANDALL. Hey Thomas...you can come out now...everyone's gone.

(**THOMAS** *is a bit concerned, but decides to show himself.*)

THOMAS. How did you know I was here?

RANDALL. I've seen you there every day for the last two weeks. You're not real good at hiding.

THOMAS. I wasn't hiding.

RANDALL. Really?

THOMAS. I...uh...was just...finishing up.

RANDALL. Finishing up, what?

THOMAS. You know, changing...I'm runnin' a little late.

RANDALL. Look, I know what you're doing.

THOMAS. You do?

RANDALL. Yeah, same thing you've been doing all semester.

THOMAS. I don't know what you're talking about.

RANDALL. You're dodgin' taking a shower.

THOMAS. What? No.

RANDALL. Come on, Thomas. We're in the same class right after gym. You're always late and you always come in sweaty.

THOMAS. Well, sometimes...

RANDALL. All times.

THOMAS. Okay, okay...I'm busted. Whatta you gonna do...call the shower police?

RANDALL. I'm not gonna call anybody. You don't want to take a shower that's your deal.

THIRD CLASS

THOMAS. Well, it probably won't be for much longer. Mr. Fowler is gettin' suspicious. He's been eyeballin' me a lot lately.

RANDALL. Just tell him.

THOMAS. What am I gonna say? "Mr. Fowler, please excuse me from taking showers because the other guys pick on me for not having any body hair yet."

RANDALL. Yeah, he's more of a bully than most of the guys in class. He'd probably make you exercise naked or something.

THOMAS. My mom thinks it's cute that I'm a "late bloomer" but it's like everybody in this school has gone through puberty except me. This is not fair.

RANDALL. Maybe she could work something out with Fowler so you don't have to shower.

THOMAS. Two problems with that. I'm embarrassed enough as it is…I don't need to add to it by dragging my mommy into it. Besides, if I tell her that everyone calls me names she'll just give me that old sticks & stones poem.

RANDALL. Yeah, I hate that.

THOMAS. So, until my body decides to catch up with everyone else's…I'll take my chances playing hide and sweat.

RANDALL. I got something better.

THOMAS. What do you mean?

RANDALL. My dad is a doctor. I'll forge you a note saying that you're not allowed to shower publicly because you have a chronic Staphylococcus Aureus infection.

THOMAS. What the heck is that?

RANDALL. Some kind of skin thing…it was on my science test last week. Fowler's a jock so he'll buy it…especially if it's from a doctor.

THOMAS. You'd do that for me?

RANDALL. Yeah, but on one condition.

THOMAS. What's that?

(reaches in his bag and pulls out a stick of deodorant)

RANDALL. Use this. I sit right behind you in class, remember?

THOMAS. You got it, man.

THOMAS. I owe you big time.

RANDALL. Just payin' it backward.

THOMAS. Backward?

RANDALL. Same thing happened to me a few years ago in junior high. I was an "early bloomer." Everyone busted on me because I had hair down there. Called me a werewolf. I went all though 7th and 8th grade dodgin' showers. Wish I would have thought of this back then. Woulda saved me a lot of grief.

THOMAS. Thanks man.

*(***RANDALL*** exits. ***THOMAS*** opens up the deodorant and starts applying it on his pits as he exits.)*

Scene Twenty-Three

(GAYLE enters with LMT – a girl who can only be seen by her. LMT stands beside GAYLE and listens attentively.)

GAYLE. When I was a child I had a lot of imaginary friends. I got rid of most of them, but I did keep one because she always tells me the real deal about what people really mean when they talk to me. I call her "Little Miss Truth." She has been an invaluable co-pilot as I navigate the confusion of lies, half-truths, and just spin doctoring that people hit me with on a daily basis.

(ERICA enters and crosses to GAYLE. ERICA cannot hear and will not respond to LMT.)

ERICA. Gayle…I've been looking all over for you.

LMT. I need something from you, as usual, because it's all about me, me, me.

ERICA. Sorry I couldn't help you with the car wash yesterday but my Mom was real sick and I had to stay home with her.

LMT. My mom is fine. I'm lazy and figured you and others would bust your butts and do the work.

GAYLE. We raised over $400 for the Senior Trip.

ERICA. That's great.

LMT. Who cares?

ERICA. You probably heard I've started to date Terrence…

LMT. If you haven't heard then let me be the first to rub it in your face since every girl in this school wants him.

GAYLE. Yes, I heard.

ERICA. Well, his cousin is going to be visiting this weekend and I thought it would be cool if you went with us to the movies.

LMT. Terrence stuck me with being a matchmaker and I need to find someone to keep his cousin occupied while we make out.

GAYLE. What does his cousin look like?

ERICA. A lot like Terrence.

LMT. If Terrance were fat, covered with zits, and had a nose the size of a zucchini.

ERICA. And he has a great personality.

LMT. He's a big jerk.

GAYLE. Why are you asking me?

ERICA. Because you're my best friend.

LMT. Because everyone else turned me down.

GAYLE. I'm pretty busy this weekend.

ERICA. Come on, it will be fun.

LMT. I'm really desperate here.

GAYLE. No, I can't. I'm sure if he looks like Terrence you'll be able to find someone with no problem.

ERICA. But I think the two of you will hit it off really well.

LMT. You're the only one I know who won't hate me forever for hooking them up with such a loser.

GAYLE. Sorry, Erica… I'm not available.

ERICA. All right, but you're missing out on the time of your life.

LMT. You're smarter than I gave you credit for.

GAYLE. My loss, see you later.

(GAYLE exits stage right. Little Miss Truth stays behind.)

ERICA. Now who am I going to get?

LMT. Where will I be able to find someone as stupid as myself?

(ERICA looks around as if she heard something, but is totally oblivious to LMT standing near her)

ERICA. *(to herself)* Stupid as myself?

(She is a bit spooked by that and exits stage left. LMT exits stage right to catch up with GAYLE)

Scene Twenty-Four

(In the darkness we see four cellphones light up for a moment before the stage lights come up. We see four students holding their phones.)

SAMANTHA. The Writer's Block Writers Club Executive Meeting is now called to order.

DARREN. Come on, Sam, do you always have to be so formal. There are only six members in our group.

DENISE. Yeah, and four of us our officers.

KATRINA. But Samantha is the President and what she says goes.

DARREN. Quit sucking up.

KATRINA. I'm not sucking up.

DARREN. My point is I think as writers we can use our own words instead of sounding like we're members of Congress or something.

DENISE. I agree.

KATRINA. So it's okay when Denise sucks up, but not me.

SAMANTHA. Enough. This is serious and I'm fine with not following meeting protocol this once.

DARREN. Good. So why are we here?

SAMANTHA. Because it's time to take a stand.

DENISE. What kind of stand?

SAMANTHA. To ditch our cellphones.

DARREN. Not that again.

SAMANTHA. We've been talking about this for two years now. And it's getting out of control. No one talks anymore. It's all texting and IM'ing and social media.

KATRINA. Yeah, and all that stupid stuff like LOL, OMG, WTF…no one is even speaking English anymore.

SAMANTHA. When's the last time you heard someone speak in a complete and intelligent sentence?

DARREN. Well, I do…and there are those besides us who speak normally. So we lead by example.

SAMANTHA. That's exactly my point. But we haven't gone far enough. We need to make a statement.

DARREN. A statement?

KATRINA. You tried that once. You wrote that op-ed in the school paper.

SAMANTHA. That didn't change anything. Most of the kids here probably didn't even read it because it was printed on paper instead of online with pretty colors and clickable links.

DARREN. There's nothing we can do to change things.

SAMANTHA. I disagree. We need to start a campaign to get rid of these…

(She holds up her cellphone.)

DENISE. What?

DARREN. Get rid of our phones? Are you insane?

SAMANTHA. Maybe, but history has proven that the craziest ideas often times make the most impact on society.

DENISE. This isn't society…it's high school.

KATRINA. I think it's a fabulous idea.

SAMANTHA. Thanks, Katrina.

KATRINA. Get rid of our phones and others will follow.

DARREN. No they won't. Besides, I need my cellphone. And I don't text that much anyway, but I do make phone calls.

DENISE. Yeah, I'd be lost without my celly.

(SAMANTHA takes out a bag.)

SAMANTHA. Desperate times call for us to take desperate measures. We need to start this campaign by showing solidarity behind it. So I want each of us to put our cellphones in this bag.

DARREN. Then what?

SAMANTHA. At the assembly tomorrow, instead of giving my honor society talk, I'm going to declare our campaign and smash our phones with a hammer!

DENISE. What?

THIRD CLASS

DARREN. What?

KATRINA. A hammer?

SAMANTHA. And then encourage everyone else to do the same. It's brilliant!

DENISE. That's not the word I would use.

SAMANTHA. All right, everybody…throw your phones in the bag. Like our forefathers who signed the Declaration of Independence…take a stand.

DARREN. Our forefathers didn't have cellphones.

DENISE. No way am I going to get rid of my phone. It took me too much begging before my parents finally got me one.

SAMANTHA. Throw it in the bag, Denise…or you are out of the club!

KATRINA. Yeah, you're out of the club.

DENISE. No problem. I've wanted to drop out of this club for a year now. I'm a writer. Writers don't work in groups.

(She exits)

SAMANTHA. Darren, the same goes for you. Stand with us… or perish.

DARREN. Perish? Really? You are so dramatic. And for a writer, that isn't even the right word.

SAMANTHA. Okay, stand with us….or…leave.

DARREN. I choose…leave.

(He exits.)

SAMANTHA. Well, Katrina, my Vice President, I know I can count on you. Free yourself.

KATRINA. Absolutely. I'm taking a stand!

(She puts her cellphone in the bag.)

SAMANTHA. We are doing something great here. Soon, others will follow, not only here, but in schools across the country.

KATRINA. We are going to change the world!

(Suddenly one of the phone rings.)

KATRINA. That's my phone…

SAMANTHA. Resist the urge, Katrina.

KATRINA. Can I just see who it is? It could be Jason. There's a rumor that he's going to ask me to the dance this weekend.

SAMANTHA. What? I heard he was going to ask me out.

(Another phone rings.)

KATRINA. That's your phone. Maybe he's calling YOU.

SAMANTHA. We have to be strong here. We have to remove temptation from our sight.

(She tosses the bag with the two phones offstage. The two phones continue to ring, the volume is even louder. **SAMANTHA** *and* **KATRINA** *are showing the pressure.)*

KATRINA. They say that one call can change your life. What if it's that one life changing call?

*(***SAMANTHA*** looks at* **KATRINA**, *they are starting to crack.)*

SAMANTHA. Okay…just this once. We'll start the movement next week.

(They both make a mad dash offstage to retrieve their phones.)

Scene Twenty-Five

*(**MASON** enters.)*

MASON. My mom has a bumper sticker on his car that says: "Violence Never Solved Anything." Now, there are many people who'd disagree with that, but my mom is what Grandpa calls a "Peacenik" like him – which I hear is some slang word old hippies like my Grandpa used to be called. Now here's the weird part. Even though my mom is non-violent and everything, after I got my butt kicked by a kid in third grade, she enrolled me in a martial arts class. I don't know if she did that because she was embarrassed or as punishment. Because for the first year while taking that class I was a walking talking bruise mark. I was put in the class to learn how to defend myself from getting my butt kicked yet I would get my butt kicked in just about every class. It took me a while to get the hang of it because I had always been more brains than muscle. But Sensei Bob didn't give up on me – I've always thought it was weird for a guy named Bob to be called Sensei – anyway, a couple years into it I was entering contests and even winning a couple. I worked my way through the belt colors and finally earned my black-belt two years ago at the age of fifteen. My mom always told me to never use my martial art skills as offense, just defense. Being a little guy, you can imagine I get picked on a lot. Well, for a while I did. Until one day in seventh grade a big mutant of a kid named Kenny went a little too far and took a swing at me while there were witnesses. That's all I needed. I proceeded to go all Jackie Chan on his face, gut, legs, and neck. Kenny cried all the way home. Like most stories that one quickly grew to ridiculousness and there are some kids here who actually believe I killed a boy by plucking out his live beating heart. Not only do the bullies at this school leave me alone, the girls think I'm hot...in a *kick everyone's butt, he's my hero* kind of way. Yes, violence never solved anything. But a few well-placed kicks and punches can make you a legend. To my fellow wimps out there I have one suggestion for you – enroll in a self-defense class early on. Because in this life it's better to be small and mighty than mighty small.

*(**BONNIE**, a cute girl, who is several inches taller than **MASON**, enters and crosses to him. She kisses him on the cheek and they exit holding hands.)*

Scene Twenty-Six

(REX is onstage. He turns to see TESS who enters.)

TESS. There you are…I've been looking all over for you.

REX. You have?

TESS. You bet I have, sexy Rexy.

(She crosses to him and starts to massage his shoulders.)

TESS. Your shoulders are so big and strong. You are such a hunk.

(HANNA enters.)

HANNA. What are you doing? Get your hands off him? He's mine.

TESS. No, he's mine and you can't have him.

(HANNA crosses to TESS and pulls her off REX, they struggle with each other. LYLE enters.)

LYLE. Hey Rex, Mr. Sennet just finished grading the final exams. You aced it!

(He hands REX a paper with a big red "A+" written on it. HANNA and TESS continue to wrestle with each other.)

REX. I didn't even study!

(ANITA enters.)

ANITA. Rex, you know that raffle ticket you bought last week? You won!

REX. What did I win?

ANITA. A new car!!!

(She hands REX some car keys.)

REX. Cool, but I'm only 14…I can't drive yet.

ANITA. Didn't you hear…they just lowered the driving age to 14? Wanna take me for a ride? I know this really romantic place.

(TESS and HANNA both rush over to ANITA.)

TESS. Hands off my property, girlie girl.

HANNA. You mean my property!

ANITA. Oh no you don't…he's mine!

(The three of them start to fight with each other. **NEAL** *enters and crosses to* **REX.***)*

REX. And what do you have for me?

NEAL. A check?

REX. How much?

NEAL. Zero. It's a reality check.

*(***NEAL** *snaps his fingers and the stage is dark. A beat later the lights come back up and* **REX** *is slumped on a cube and the others are all gone;* **NEAL** *stands next to him and gives him a shake.)*

NEAL. Rex, wake up.

REX. *(wakens)* Huh?

NEAL. You fell asleep on the bus.

REX. Is school over?

NEAL. No, it's Monday morning. Let's go …if you're late for class again you're lookin' at detention.

*(***NEAL** *heads off.* **REX** *is stunned and starts to follow.)*

REX. Life is so cruel!

(He exits.)

Scene Twenty-Seven

(LAURA enters holding a bouquet of flowers and wearing a beauty pageant sash.)

LAURA. I won my first beauty contest when I was only 2 years old: the "Little Miss Sweetheart Competition." I don't remember anything about it, but my Mother made sure that there were plenty of pictures and saved all the newspaper clippings. And so started what has become a long history of contests and pageants. All the time I hated the whole scene – the dresses, the smiling, the judges, the ugly trophies. But I knew it would break my Mother's heart if I told her I wanted no part of it. You see, she was the one winning those contests, not me. I saw it in her face every time they announced my name. She was the one up on the stage. The flowers, the applause, the attention, they were all for her. She said that it was part of the big plan to make me somebody...which was really crazy because I already considered myself somebody. *(pause)* Next week, I'm featured in "Ski World" magazine as "Miss Ski Teen-Bunny." This is going to stop. That sort of image just doesn't work for a pediatrician, which is what I want to be. *(takes off her sash)* And I'm going to tell her: No more beauty contests, no more photo shoots, no more of all of this. I love my Mother, but she's going to have to look somewhere else for her dreams. And may God have mercy on my little sister.

(She exits, tossing the flowers aside.)

Scene Twenty-Eight

(JESSIE *paces nervously for a few moments. Finally she spots* LANA *who enters; crosses up to her.*)

JESSIE. You were in there long enough.

LANA. Not that long.

JESSIE. Over 45 minutes.

LANA. You didn't have to wait.

JESSIE. So what happened?

LANA. Not what you thought was going to happen.

JESSIE. There's no way Hansen's gonna let you do that speech at graduation.

LANA. I don't think he was as shocked by it as you were.

JESSIE. I wasn't shocked.

LANA. Yes you were. You told me that my words were… "flammable."

JESSIE. You're the valedictorian of the class. You're supposed to say happy and positive things. He insisted on that, right?

LANA. John is really not that narrow minded of a guy.

JESSIE. John? You called the Principal of this school by his first name?

LANA. He told me to.

JESSIE. What? I thought you were gonna get reamed…and he tells you to call him John! *(pause)* That must have been before he read your speech.

LANA. No…he had already read it.

JESSIE. This is totally incredible. So you get to read it as is! All right, we're gonna have some fireworks at our graduation!

LANA. Not exactly.

JESSIE. Okay…here we go. I knew this was too good to be true. What really happened?

LANA. It's just like I told you. He read it. We talked about it. He made some valid points. He talked about the tradition of commencement and how all the parents will be there and families. He explained that certain things in my speech would no doubt...how did he put it... "ruffle some feathers."

JESSIE. That's censorship!

LANA. Hold on, don't jump to conclusions. *(pause)* I listened to what he had to say. I then went through my speech, point by point, and explained to him why I felt I needed to say these things. That it's how I feel and how I thought that this was the forum to express my feelings.

JESSIE. And he tried to talk you out of it. That's what took so long, right?

LANA. As a matter of fact he understood my position.

JESSIE. Iron Hand Hansen understood your position?

LANA. Like I said, he's not the monster you make him out to be.

JESSIE. That I make him out to be?

LANA. All right, I've called him the same thing...in the past. But not after today.

JESSIE. Meaning?

LANA. He told me that I could do the entire speech...as is. That I had earned the right. And he would defend my right to give it, no matter what happens.

JESSIE. No way.

LANA. Surprised me too.

JESSIE. So you get to give your speech. It's really gonna knock some people on their butts. Major fireworks!

LANA. Maybe not.

JESSIE. What do you mean?

LANA. I'm going to give the speech, but I'm going to make a few changes. I think there's still a way to say what I want without offending people.

JESSIE. Sheesh, Iron Hand does it again.

LANA. No, I told you he said it was okay to do it, as is. He doesn't even know I'm going to change it.

JESSIE. So why are you changing it?

LANA. Because he treated me like an adult. He stood behind my rights even though it's going to give him a lot of grief.

JESSIE. I don't understand.

LANA. I'm not sure I do, either. But something inside tells me I learned a lot more in that meeting than I have in all of my classes that got me to this point.

(LANA starts to leave.)

JESSIE. Where you going?

LANA. Home…to make some changes. Maybe even to rewrite the whole thing.

JESSIE. Rewrite the whole thing? This makes no sense!

LANA. It makes all the sense in the world. Come on… I'll explain it to you on the way home.

JESSIE. But what about graduation? What about some fireworks?

LANA. I guess you're just going to have to bring your own, Jessie.

JESSIE. I don't believe this…

(LANA exits and JESSIE follows after her.)

Scene Twenty-Nine

(Music up "Pomp and Circumstance" plays. **BRIAN** *and* **JESSICA** *– from the first scene – enter. They are both dressed in graduation caps and gowns.)*

JESSICA. I hate that I'm going to be the last person in line to get my diploma.

BRIAN. Not your fault your last name is Zelman?

JESSICA. My dad will crack on me about it meaning I was the bottom of our class.

BRIAN. You got accepted at a good college…that puts you ahead of a lot of seniors.

JESSICA. That wouldn't impress him. He expected as much.

BRIAN. Hey, it's your life now. Don't worry about it.

JESSICA. You don't know my dad.

BRIAN. If it will help…trade places with me. Then you won't be last.

JESSICA. No, they're doing it alphabetically…that will just confuse everyone.

BRIAN. My dad is relieved I made it this far. Most parents here brought their video camera…mine hired a film crew.

JESSICA. Those are for you? I thought someone was doing a documentary or something.

BRIAN. Yeah, I think he's going to call it "Brian Graduated High School: The Final Sign of the Apocalypse."

JESSICA. You're the smartest guy I know. Street smart anyway.

BRIAN. Too bad there aren't any scholarships for that.

JESSICA. I thought you said you're going to college.

BRIAN. Junior College. That means I'll be living at home. It's like being in the 13th grade.

JESSICA. Oh.

BRIAN. I heard Phillips was going to go naked under his gown and flash everyone when he gets his diploma.

JESSICA. I saw him. He's wearing a suit like everybody else.

BRIAN. Coward. Bet no one is wearing a suit like mine.

(**BRIAN** *opens up his gown to reveal he is wearing a bathing suit.*)

JESSICA. No way.

BRIAN. I started the school year this way...and I'm going to end it this way. I only have three months, four days, 12 hours and 23 minutes before I have to report to J.C. and I intend to enjoy every last second of it. *(beat)* I know, I know...you think I'm crazy.

JESSICA. Not really.

(**JESSICA** *opens her gown revealing that she is wearing a bathing suit underneath.*)

BRIAN. Whoa...Nice!

JESSICA. I've been thinking about this ever since the first day of school when I saw you in the courtyard. I want to enjoy every last second, too. *(fetching)* And I want to enjoy it with you.

BRIAN. Cool. If we leave right after the ceremony we can be at the beach before sundown.

JESSICA. What about our parents?

BRIAN. They'll get the money shot when we get our diplomas. That's all they really care about.

(*The music gets louder.*)

JESSICA. We'd better hurry or we're going to miss getting them.

(**BRIAN** *takes* **JESSICA**'s *hand and they exit.*)

Scene Thirty

(STEVEN enters and sets up his tripod. He removes his camera from a bag and begins to mount it on the tripod. MELANIE enters.)

MELANIE. There you are. I've been looking all over for you...

STEVEN. Well, you found me.

MELANIE. What are you doing?

STEVEN. Setting up my last shot of the year.

MELANIE. Last shot?

STEVEN. In five minutes the last class of the last day of school lets out for everyone except the Seniors who have already graduated. I want to capture the excitement and hysteria of the student body as they are released from their cells and into the free world... well for a summer anyway.

MELANIE. Steven, we finished our video yearbook last week.

STEVEN. I know. I was the one that edited it and made all those copies.

MELANIE. Right. Just about every kid in this school bought one.

STEVEN. I know...

MELANIE. So why are you setting up a shot?

STEVEN. Force of habit I guess. You had me film so much stuff...I just thought I should get the last day, too. Maybe I'll make a sequel.

MELANIE. You did a great job...your editing was brilliant. Everybody loved it. We made a fortune. And now it's time to reap the rewards of our hard work.

(She reaches in her purse and pulls out an envelope. Hands it to him.)

MELANIE. Your half. And a lot more than I had predicted.

*(**STEVEN** opens the envelope and pulls a check out.)*

STEVEN. *(looks at check)* This is not right.

(He hands the check back to her.)

MELANIE. It's exactly right. I'll show you the accounting. I didn't cheat you…

STEVEN. Didn't say you did.

MELANIE. Then what's the problem?

STEVEN. What's not right is that with your business and marketing skills you should have gotten a scholarship instead of me.

MELANIE. You got a scholarship?

STEVEN. Thanks to you?

MELANIE. Me?

STEVEN. My dad watched the DVD we made. For the first time I can ever remember he was actually impressed with something I did. He even used the "P" word.

MELANIE. Perfect?

STEVEN. Proud. So much so he overnighted a copy to my uncle in Cali who is somehow connected with a big film school there. He loved it…and was so blown away he arranged for me to get a full ride in their program.

MELANIE. That's amazing.

STEVEN. So thanks to you…you've already paid me my share. You keep that.

MELANIE. Really? You sure?

STEVEN. For someone who loves to direct…you don't take direction very well.

MELANIE. I don't know what to say.

STEVEN. Say you'll study hard. I'm going to need a business manager after I start making big Hollywood blockbuster movies.

*(**MELANIE** puts it back in her bag and then gives him a big hug. It is interrupted by the sound of a school bell.)*

STEVEN. Here we go.

(The rest of the student cast explodes onto the stage with the excitement that can only come from the last day of classes. They all start to notice the camera. **MELANIE**

crosses to them and organizes a group shot. They form a tableau for the camera.)

STEVEN. Okay everybody. Starting from left to right I want you to say one word that sums up this past year at school. Ready...action!

(This is ad-libbed by your student cast. Each cast member will say one word of their choice to sum up how they feel about the school year. After everyone has said their word...)

STEVEN. And now I'm going to say the two favorite words of high school students everywhere... "Class dismissed!"

(The students cheer as they exit the stage, talking excitedly as they go. And, of course, the lights fade out.)

The End